# BREAKING
# POINTS

# BREAKING
# POINTS

## Chelsea Stickle

BLACK LAWRENCE PRESS

 Black
Lawrence
Press

www.blacklawrence.com

Executive Editor: Diane Goettel
Chapbook Editor: Kit Frick
Book and Cover Design: Zoe Norvell

Published 2021 by Black Lawrence Press.
Printed in the United States.

*For all the people who taught me how to walk away.*

# Table of Contents

# What the Detectives Found in Her Abandoned Car

The guts of a dead mosquito on the inside of the windshield. Smashed by the recently rolled *Elle* on the passenger side floor. A can of OFF! rolling around next to it.

A hole in the dashboard where the cigarette lighter should be. An empty pack of Marlboros. Husband says she quit for the baby. Gave birth a month ago. The baby's at his sister's.

The car key hidden in the visor.

A holstered taser in the armrest compartment. A pill bottle— the label neatly peeled off—crammed with quarters. A packet of ladybug tissues. An iPhone charger. A first aid kit. A tartan wool blanket. An empty, unused gasoline container. A flashlight. Reusable grocery bags. An umbrella. Wet wipes: used and unused. Annie's bunny snack wrappers crinkled under the seats. Crumpled Safeway receipts as long as her arm.

A child's drawing of the family in front of their house. Stick figures holding stick hands. A pregnant woman. A child with blue hair. A man towering over them.

Scatterings of loose soil and woodchips on the backseat floor. The husband explains that these aren't clues. She buys indoor plants, kills them, and replaces them regularly. And she never cleans her car. Inside or out. She always waits for the next rainstorm. He repeats his insistence that they interrogate the neighbor who eyed his wife's belly. The boss who sat on her desk and played with his balls. A detective tells him now is the time for collecting evidence. The car is in front of them. It needs to be examined for leads.

When CSI searches for blood, they find none. In fact, there are no signs of a struggle at all. The husband doesn't understand. A new mother would never. His wife would never.

It's like she stepped out of the car and walked until she reached something. The sea air with her toes enmeshed in wet sand. A cave that echoed so she could finally hear herself. The quiet solitude of the dwarfing Redwood forest with trunks the size of cars. The past smaller than a speck behind her.

# Coming of Age

It's weird seeing her cut off at the waist in a glass box. A mannequin in an upright coffin disguised as an arcade game is always going to be strange, even if there is a crystal ball by her hand. It costs one dollar to hear my fortune. I never play.

We're not even supposed to be in here—Christina and I, not alone anyway. My older sister Elise is supposed to be watching us, but all she wants to do is sunbathe on a beach towel until she smells like peanut butter. She tells us we can do whatever we want as long as we stay together. We lick cotton candy off our fingers, or rig a dollar on some line to fish for rednecks on the pier. When we overheat we hide out in the arcade.

The arcade is one of the few places where there are only other kids, usually all boys, sometimes high schoolers. We're not old enough to be noticed by boys yet. Elise saunters in and every eye is on her. Christina and I walk in and nobody cares, which is great. I'd be happy avoiding all that for the rest of my life.

Christina doesn't understand. This summer she started plucking her eyebrows into thin lines and dutifully applying watermelon lip gloss in store windows. She sees our inability to get noticed as failure, so she tries harder.

I'm staring at the fortune teller game as she showily struggles with pinball when a boy about two years older appears. "Not having any luck?"

Christina pouts and sticks her chest out. "None."

"Let me show you," he says but doesn't wait for permission. He snakes his arms around her as she blushes and glances at me, looking for outside confirmation that it's actually happening.

I cross my arms and watch them play a tired game. Everything he says or does is wonderful, and she's so grateful to learn from such a master. She's never played this game before, but she's seen enough movies to know her lines. When he's imparted all of his wisdom, he steps back. She takes a half-step toward him, so he can see down her spaghetti strap tank top.

"Nice tits," he says.

Her eyes turn down for the full effect of her falsies as her shoulder spasms into a shrug. "Thanks."

He leers at me and says, "You'd probably have nice tits, too, if you didn't hide 'em."

Christina giggles.

My arms tighten over my sweatshirt. She's betrayed me for some boy we met three minutes ago because he makes her feel pretty. "We should go," I say, yanking her toward the exit.

"Wait," she says to me, and simpers back at him.

He trails us outside. There's a group of boys in a circle. They shout at the boy, who flips them off. "Hey, I've got an idea," he says. "Let's go watch the sunset. I know a place."

Christina rips her hand from mine and scratches my palms with her homemade French manicure. My hand falls limply to my side. She's talked about moments like this. She pictures her first kiss against the most romantic setting imaginable—a sunset.

She pats the tube of lip gloss in the back pocket of her short shorts but knows she can't re-apply without him seeing, and he has to know her lips are naturally sticky sweet. "Great!"

He seizes her hand and they start off. I numbly follow.

"Sonya, you can't come," Christina chastises.

I stop moving. Stranger danger doesn't disappear when you start wearing a push-up bra. "We're not supposed to go anywhere alone."

He glances at Christina critically for the first time. Her perfect kiss begins to slip away. "She's just kidding," Christina says. "I can go wherever I want."

"Well you're not alone if you're with me," he says.

It's the smoothest line Christina's ever heard. She hits the side of her breast against him and gazes up at him like he's a god.

"Keep an eye on her!" he calls to the group of boys, who perk up and come over.

I'm suddenly aware that there aren't any other people near us and that no one knows where we are. My blood soars through my veins. "Christina!" I plead.

"Come on, it'll be fun," she calls back. "You get your pick."

The Axe body spray masking BO announces the presence of the five boys as they swarm me. Being so outnumbered, I don't like my odds. I know what happens next. I've seen movies, too. I can hear their lewd thoughts and sense their sticky fingers. I don't wait to learn more.

I run until my lungs ache. I run until I taste iron on my tongue and my thighs are stiff. I swerve into the dunes and onto the populated beach. It's the safest place I can think of. I don't glance behind until I splash into the water. The coolness drifts over my flip flops and the sand slurps them up. Bending over, I press my sweaty, scratched palms onto my knees and suck air into my mouth like a dying fish.

The boys are gone but so is Christina.

# We're Not Allowed Outside

Because of the DC sniper, I get my first cell phone. A Nokia with impossibly small buttons. When I look up, my parents' smiles are even faker than the ones in family photos. I'm twelve. Old enough to know they want me to be able to call for help. Last year was 9/11. We live sixteen miles from the Pentagon, and the CIA is around the corner. Ever since 9/11 we hold our breaths when we drive past Langley. Everyone's afraid that's next. But we're wrong. This year some guy is shooting kids for sport.

My middle school changes its protocol. We're not allowed outside. We play board games inside for recess. PE is in the gym. We get on buses to leave, but once they drop us off, we have to find somewhere indoors if no one's arrived yet. The woman organizing my carpool tells us to hide out in Popeyes if she's late. The other adults agree. We're like chicks being herded, peeping, one wrong move away from the fryer.

We get used to it: staying indoors, looking over our shoulders, avoiding white box vans and listening for the sound of a car backfiring. We don't huddle together. It'd only make us a bigger target. We stay home and watch TV. Call each other and make plans for when this is all over. The radio in Mom's car says it hasn't even been a full month, but it feels like forever.

Then one day they catch the guys. They weren't in a white box van, after all. I don't listen to the news. There's no sense in killing people pumping gas. Nothing to be learned. I play Snake on my phone. We go back to soccer practice. Wait at the bus stop for our parents. We don't get murdered. We're lucky.

Mom says she needs to pick up something and parks at the edge of a Home Depot lot. There's a hardware store down the street from our house. I don't know why we're all the way out here. It's late afternoon, but it's winter so it's dark already. She tells me the sniper shot someone here, that she died on her way in. The shadows created by the overhang become sharper. I can just picture an ordinary woman running an errand and disappearing from the world in a pool of her own blood.

Mom hasn't moved. She takes a breath, a moment, and sits still. Her face is impassive. I can't see fear or excitement or anything beyond an unfamiliar blankness. I reach out and feel her frozen fingers like individual icicles. Each colder than the last. The windows fog until the outside world is obscured, immense and unknowable. We can only see what's right in front of us.

# Through Rose-Colored Glasses

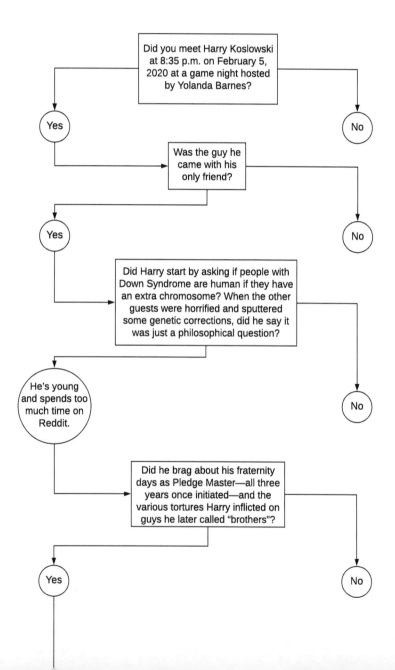

Did you meet Harry Koslowski at 8:35 p.m. on February 5, 2020 at a game night hosted by Yolanda Barnes?

Yes

No

Was the guy he came with his only friend?

Yes

No

Did Harry start by asking if people with Down Syndrome are human if they have an extra chromosome? When the other guests were horrified and sputtered some genetic corrections, did he say it was just a philosophical question?

He's young and spends too much time on Reddit.

No

Did he brag about his fraternity days as Pledge Master—all three years once initiated—and the various tortures Harry inflicted on guys he later called "brothers"?

Yes

No

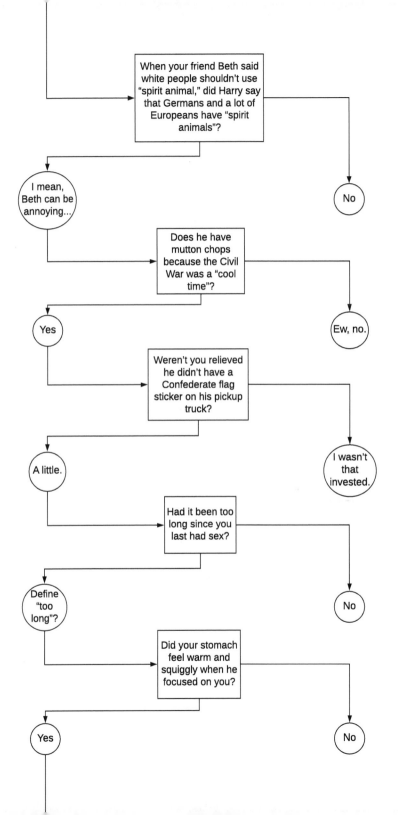

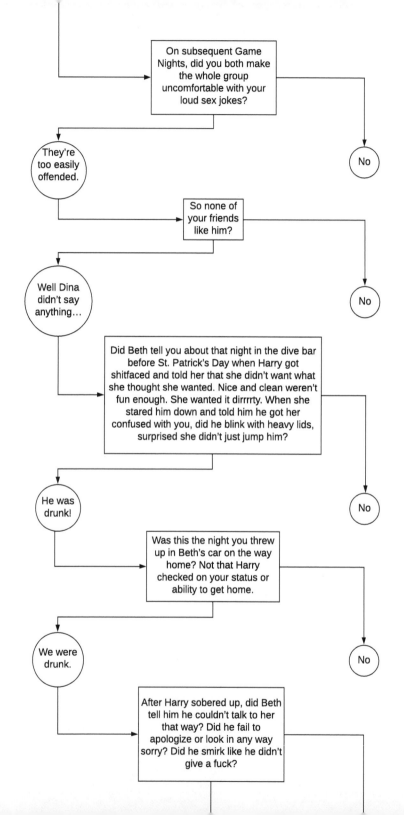

On subsequent Game Nights, did you both make the whole group uncomfortable with your loud sex jokes?

No

They're too easily offended.

So none of your friends like him?

No

Well Dina didn't say anything…

Did Beth tell you about that night in the dive bar before St. Patrick's Day when Harry got shitfaced and told her that she didn't want what she thought she wanted. Nice and clean weren't fun enough. She wanted it dirrrrty. When she stared him down and told him he got her confused with you, did he blink with heavy lids, surprised she didn't just jump him?

No

He was drunk!

Was this the night you threw up in Beth's car on the way home? Not that Harry checked on your status or ability to get home.

No

We were drunk.

After Harry sobered up, did Beth tell him he couldn't talk to her that way? Did he fail to apologize or look in any way sorry? Did he smirk like he didn't give a fuck?

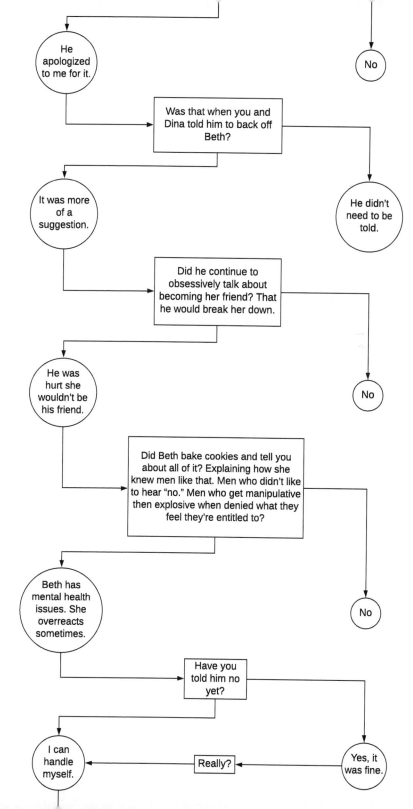

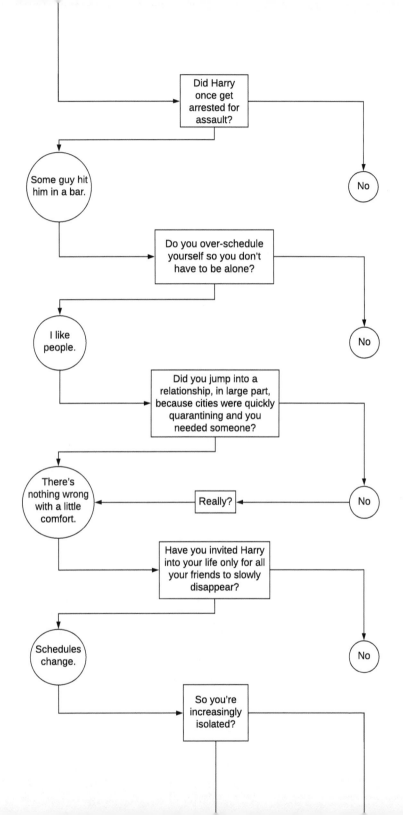

Did Harry once get arrested for assault?

No

Some guy hit him in a bar.

Do you over-schedule yourself so you don't have to be alone?

No

I like people.

Did you jump into a relationship, in large part, because cities were quickly quarantining and you needed someone?

No

There's nothing wrong with a little comfort.

Really?

Have you invited Harry into your life only for all your friends to slowly disappear?

No

Schedules change.

So you're increasingly isolated?

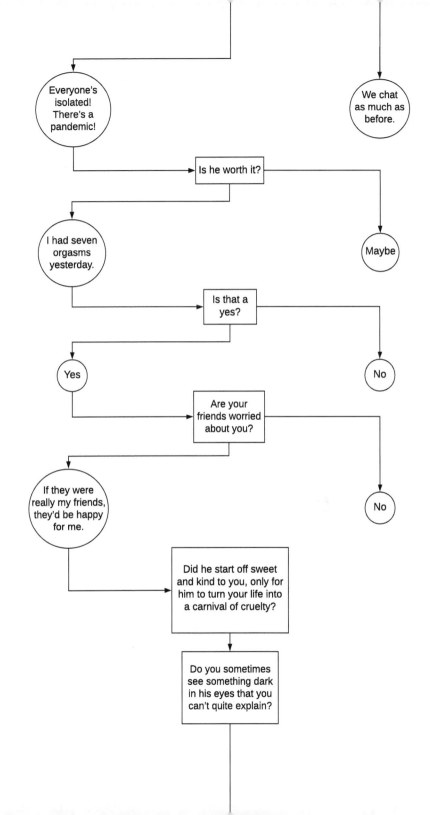

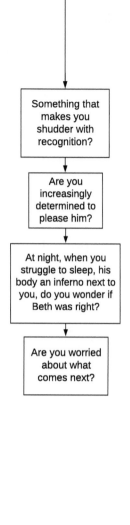

Something that makes you shudder with recognition?

Are you increasingly determined to please him?

At night, when you struggle to sleep, his body an inferno next to you, do you wonder if Beth was right?

Are you worried about what comes next?

# The One Who Gets Away

You are the one who gets away. The one who doesn't accept that drink she didn't see get made, provoking the dude in the backward baseball cap to scream, "I'm not a rapist!" You never said he was but now you've got suspicions. You are the one who gets a bad vibe from those guys in the dive bar, like they're all gripping the wooden handles of steel knives to press against the thin skin on your neck, and it has you calling an Uber instead of shoving your tongue down the ginger's throat. You're the one watching the placement of their hands and observing the thin veneer of civility they fake before they can reveal the fur and canines of the end-less-stomached wolf beneath. You will not be their dinner tonight.

You make it home okay. You don't get roofied or raped. You don't wake up wondering where your underwear is. You're one of the lucky ones. The adrenaline of having narrowly escaped a clos-ing cage keeps you up past when the other girls stumble home, eyeliner smeared and unclear about what happened. Shaking off their discomfort and the tiny voices in their heads by confirming via text that it was awesome! So much fun! If only it weren't for you. They call you a worrywart to your face and a stuck-up, no-fun bitch behind it.

They stop inviting you out. No one wants a reminder of the fragility of their bodies. The unimportance of their volition. Or how easily their autonomy can be snatched away by some no-named rando on a whim. All they want is oblivion. To forget their student loan debt and the ever-louder ticking of their biological clock for an hour or two. You are too intense, too real, too pulsing. Ignoring reality has only ever given you a ruptured appendix when you were twelve. But your reality checks, like the one that kept you alive, harsh their buzz.

You would've had to block out that night for one reason or another. You chose the one where you find out who your friends really are. You didn't even realize it was a choice. The small voice of self-protection in the back of your head was momentarily louder than your desire to get along and be cool. But you've never been cool. You've never been willing to make the sacrifice.

# How to Make Stock with Thanksgiving Leftovers

1.  On Thursday night after the turkey's cooled, rip every shred of meat from the carcass. Ignore your distant relatives' complaints that you're wasting valuable family time. Don't tell them that's the point, that you barely made it through the door this year after what they did to your now ex-girlfriend Kerry at Christmas.

2.  Dislocate the thighs and wings. In fact, separate as many bones as you can. Take pleasure in the snap of cartilage. Twist bones to weaken joints. Experience the primal satisfaction of taking apart an animal. Don't picture your smug uncle asking if Kerry's "the girl" as you do this.

3.  Bag all the bones. Don't call anyone a bag of bones. If you struggle to get the entire chest cavity in, don't be afraid to crush the ribs. Enjoy the light snaps. Ignore your relatives as they watch—horrified—as your forearms and stomach get sprayed with meat, fat, and viscera. Reality makes them queasy.

4.  Wash your hands three times with scalding water, up and down your forearms. You're washing your hands of them. You won't get guilted into Christmas. Not when your cousin Greg never apologized for cupping Kerry's ass and promising he could turn her straight. Not that your family believed it.

5.  Toss the bones into a stock pot. Add vegetables and season it. Rosemary and thyme for depth. Salt to bring out the range

of flavors. Peppercorns for spiciness. Then add six cups of cold water. Cover the bones.

6.  Bring to a boil. Don't focus on all the digs at your lack of a dress, your lack of makeup, and your lack of a partner. Don't think about their belief that people like you shouldn't be allowed to adopt. Hell, they voted for the guy who thinks you belong in conversion therapy. The water will be boiling in no time.

7.  Cover and let simmer for an hour and thirty minutes. Listen as Greg's children run willy-nilly throughout the house, breaking the occasional heirloom, and balk when his wife tries to smear her lipstick on you. It's not like lipstick saved her.

8.  Lift the lid to give your simmering stock a stir. Feel your rage hum in your throat, growing with every pity-filled look from the people who are supposed to love you, and every dig that's designed to make you rethink your choices. As the hum threatens to burst from your throat, feel your mother's hand on your shoulder as she offers you a mug of steaming peppermint tea and offers a sympathetic look. She's why you're still here. She's the one that matters to you. But she's also the one who says and does nothing to help you, lets your relatives tear you apart until there's nothing left. Waited almost a year and then criticized Kerry for reacting to the abuse you're accustomed to. The one who says, "Don't be so sensitive!" when you complain. Understand that you don't need them anymore for food and shelter like you did when you were a kid.

9.  When the liquid is golden, remove the bones, vegetables, and seasoning. Skim and toss the fat that comes to the surface. In lieu of proper storage, bags will do. Call Great-Aunt Jean an old bag and fill it with stock.

10. The stock bag lasts up to two months in the freezer. Pain from relatives can last a lifetime. Feel the warm-in-your-belly soup made from scraps that radiates through your extremities, warmer than your family any day of the year.

# Though Her Teeth Never Break Skin

Here's how it works. She asks a question, all friendly, like she's still trying to get to know me after over a year of being close. Based on my last few friendship catastrophes, I decided to always be upfront and honest. Stand up straight and tell the truth. Assuming I'm not a total asshole about it, any problem is either coming from their side or is a conversation we can have.

So when we're together she asks about my life. They're just questions. Like, *Do you wish you'd had a sibling?* Or, *Do you think your childhood would've been better if you'd had a sibling?* Under the cover of her cousin considering a second child. They're leading questions designed to make me reconsider my position on my life story. I mean, it might've been nice to have someone to compare notes with. I was the only witness. Parts of me break off like the segments of a chocolate bar. The little shavings between sections melt and make tiny messes if you just know where to look. There are no physical scars, so what if it was all in my head? And the thing I don't say, pressing it to my chest behind laced fingers like it's an enormous, faceted ruby, because some things are just for me: I always wanted an older brother to defend me and keep me safe from my parents.

Her frosty blue eyes are locked on the table. A small smile seesaws across her mouth while I squirm. This is fun for her. She's enjoying my pain. Thriving on it. Because it means she's not alone.

My regular trauma—the stuff I've talked about and processed—it's not enough anymore. She needs fresh pain.

I'm not used to anyone giving a fuck about me. I'm the one who listens while people, unprompted, unburden themselves. But it's starting to occur to me that this is not what's supposed to happen. I'm not supposed to feel like my strength is being sucked from my body with every follow-up question until I'm the husk of the person I was five minutes ago while she rubs her belly, full of my blood she stole, even though her teeth never broke the skin.

# Household Extractions

I'm wiggling my loosest front tooth when Mom oh-so-casually says, "I think it's really unattractive when front teeth come in separately. Remember Sally Treem? Wouldn't it be nice if both of your front teeth came in together?"

Every time Mom gets an idea, she gets this glint of desire in her sharp blue eyes and a smirk on her permanently lipsticked mouth. It's like she's going to a carnival, but I never know if I get to sit next to her or become part of the ride. She's glinting and smirking and I know this time, I'm the ride.

"You'd be so much prettier." Disagreement isn't an option. There wasn't really a question in the first place. Mom only says one thing to get to another, forever leading me down a dark rabbit hole. "If you want, I can help you and pull them out."

The sunlight streaming through the casement windows makes her nail polish look shiny, like fresh blood. The noxious fumes of nail polish and remover forever assault me. She paints them in the car, in front of the TV, at her vanity. I try to remember when she last painted them, if the polish will wrinkle and catch on the ridges of my teeth like a discarded second skin. Underneath, her nails are yellow from the decades of dye that turned them into talons.

When I say, "I guess," she leads me upstairs to her bed and gets me to lie down. She straddles me and starts pulling on the looser one. Her finger pads are on either side, and I taste nail polish remover. My tooth's not loose enough, but she's diligent, determined to take it with her.

"Keep your neck back," she says as my head follows my tooth for the tenth time. Tears drip from the corners of my eyes. Enough force and the root snaps, leaving a trail of blood drops across her pillow. Mom triumphantly holds up my front tooth. I run my tongue over the empty grave in my mouth and it's pulpy, bloody, fresh.

"Now for the next one."

The next one is barely wiggling. Mom exerts more force, invigorated by her recent victory. I don't know if it's possible to have bruised gums, but I can feel one blooming under her care. Agony radiates from the front of my mouth. I moan and writhe, always aware of the blood trail just out of the corner of my eye. "Let me finish," she says through a clenched jaw.

I freeze my body and step outside of it. The pain becomes an echo of itself. I forget who I am. I notice the detail in the metalwork headboard of my parents' bed. How every surface is mirrored. The soft, plush carpet like a pink sea around me, one that won't save me on this rocking ship.

The second tooth appears in Mom's hand. My gum vibrates, and my tongue gravitates to the empty space. The iron of my blood is sharp, must fill the gap where my teeth were.

Mom rinses and dries off my bloody teeth before dropping them into the oval-shaped Limoges box where she keeps the rest of my baby teeth. She tries to protect them from the porcelain by including a tissue for padding, but the high-pitched clinking is unmistakable. The mother bunny on top of the box glares at me.

"Would you like some ice cream?" she asks. "I think we have chocolate chip."

I nod, afraid of my voice, and she leaves me alone in a room that feels devoid of all humanity, like no one's ever been here but me, sinking into the duvet and the bloody pillow. And I vanish.

# Heirloom Seed Propagation

When she was five, Lydia buried a strawberry in the yard under the freshly laid mulch. Her puffy pink Easter dress and the patent white leather Mary Janes got dirty, but Lydia thought it was better than telling her grandmother that strawberries are too sour. Strawberries were the closest thing her grandmother had to a family crest. She had strawberry hand towels, strawberry soap, strawberry dessert plates for the strawberry shortcake, and Lydia's mother had stressed the importance of saying yes to everything her grandmother offered her. That's what kept everyone calm. Her mother hadn't said she had to eat everything, though. So the ground swallowed what Lydia rejected. Mounds and mounds of strawberries.

The strawberry patches encircled her grandmother's backyard. She called it providence. Lydia called it fecal seed distribution. It was one of the main ways seeds were propagated. An animal ate something and shit it out where a plant eventually grew. Her mother glared at her. Lydia was always getting in trouble for telling the truth these days. It suited her conscience but made her stomach ache. Some people you have to walk on eggshells around, and some people it's broken pieces of pottery that slice your feet open with nicks and gashes until you're so bloody that your feet don't look like feet anymore. Just amorphous blobs of blood, bone, and meat.

"Are you sure you want that chocolate cake?" her grandmother asked. "A moment on the lips is a lifetime on the hips!" She held up the big, juicy strawberry coated in sugar on her fork. "These strawberries are so fresh!"

What her grandmother meant: you're fat, if you're not careful you'll get fatter and then no one will ever want you and what will you do?

Lydia yanked down her shirt, afraid some skin might be showing. She wore everything at least a size too big because she didn't like the way people looked at her, always categorizing her as fuckable or competition or not worthy of basic respect. "I like this cake," she said and forced in a mouthful.

"Chocolate is bad for your skin."

"Actually that's a myth," Lydia said through a full mouth. "It's sugar spikes that do it, and sugar can come from anything. Even strawberries." She'd contradicted her grandmother with facts. A no-no since she learned to speak. The momentary pleasure gave way to dread.

Her grandmother set down her fork. Her eyes were stormy and her face had turned into a perfect mask of disgust the way Paul Ekman described it in *Unmasking the Face*. Nose lifted, raised cheeks and a lifted upper lip. Her grandmother couldn't challenge her on the facts, so she went to her only two avenues of expertise: appearance and men. "Why are you so pale?"

Translation: fix your face, being tan is attractive, why are you so ugly?

"I don't know," Lydia said. "Maybe because I don't work outside?"

Her grandmother pursed her lips. Their family's American origins were in the dairy farm she'd grown up running.

Lydia shoved more cake into her mouth and grinned. She never won.

Her grandmother's ninetieth birthday was attended by the whole family. Lydia even came down from Amherst at her mother's request. Her grandmother screeched out who should sit where and tried to offer her wine. She read her grandmother's intentions to get her drunk and declined.

"Do you have a boyfriend?" her grandmother asked, like she always did. She had never asked what classes Lydia took or what the campus was like. Lydia was a nerd in a family of wannabe beauty queens because beauty was power. If she'd been a boy, she would've been hailed as the family scholar. As a girl she was a failed girlfriend/future wife. That suited her just fine.

"No," Lydia said.

"Do you have any male teachers?"

Lydia swallowed her desire to scream about abuse of power. How she would never compromise her education that way. Men come and go. Her education couldn't be taken from her. Even though all of her teachers were male that semester, she said, "No."

After dinner, the family set about the strawberry patches with wicker baskets to pick dessert. Lydia was in charge of picking for her grandmother and made sure she selected the ones with white peeking from beneath the green tops. She believed they were the sourest.

In the photo series from that day, Lydia can be seen standing next to her grandmother, as pale as ever, having spent more time inside with books than with boys on the lawn. Her smile is forced, patient, waiting for the day it doesn't have to pretend.

When Lydia's grandmother died, her mother hired people to clean, toss, and donate what was left of her life. The house was empty when Lydia arrived. She retrieved the brand-new shovel from her trunk. She stomped the blade into the earth until her feet blistered and her hands stung. It took an hour, but she dug up every single root that could've given life to a strawberry. Her stomach aches were gone. Joy sprouted from her body like a second skin. She bagged the plants to take to the dump and left the holes in the ground. Some things weren't meant to be filled.

# Quiz: How Mature Are You?

*Circle the answer that best fits your response. Be honest!*

**1. When a co-worker steals your lunch, you:**

A) Emit a guttural scream. Ask what man committed this crime! Lecture the entire office on boundaries. Your bark is worse than your bite, but they don't know that.

B) Hunt down the motherfucker who ate your pastrami sandwich! Tell him to keep his hand at the level of his eye when he walks to the parking garage tonight.

C) Go home. Take a nap under a blanket fort.

D) Find the person eating your lunch and tell him that if he wanted you to make him a sandwich, all he had to do was ask! You'd be more than happy to pack for two sometimes! Maybe Fridays?

E) Remind everyone that you labeled your lunch. For the next few days go out to eat. Watch the thief wither without your delicious food.

**2. When that bitch in your book club calls you a space cadet, you:**

A) Tell her to fuck off. You know you want to! You've been so patient with her hater ass. You deserve a little release!

B) Stab her hand with a fork. Shatter a metacarpal. Feel how your ancestors must have felt when they conquered worlds.

C) Freeze and replay everything you've ever said or done that could make her think that. Sift through hours and hours of footage. By the time you remember you're in a room full of people, no one remembers what she said.

D) Tell her she's right! You are totally spacey. You should probably work on that.

E) Ignore her. This can look like C, but it's intentional.

**3. When a friend asks for help moving even though she knows you have back problems, you:**

A) Call her a shitty friend. Why can't she remember the basics about you! What is wrong with her?

B) Slap her until she remembers that you're always in pain.

C) Tell her you're busy that day.

D) Help her and injure yourself but don't say anything. Spend hundreds of dollars on chiropractor treatments just to get back to your normal pain level.

E) Remind her that you can't lift. Offer to bring bagels or lunch to make her move more enjoyable.

**4. When your mother obsesses over the weight you've gained since your high school graduation fifteen years ago, you:**

A) Call her a bitch. Who else would randomly talk about your body without prompting? Tell her we can't all have eating disorders, Karen.

B) It's mostly muscle. Cardio kickboxing is going really well. Tell her that the next time you see her you can kick her ass until she gets the right idea.

C) Say nothing. You can feel your healthy dinner rapidly putrefying in your stomach. But it's a free country. You can't tell her what she can and can't say. That would be fascist. She's entitled to her opinion. Even when it makes you cry in the shower before work.

D) Tell her she's right. You have gained weight, but you're working on it. Going to the gym five days a week and eating healthy. Your body changed. You're trying to do better.

E) You didn't ask for her opinion, and you don't want it. Tell her if she can't say anything nice, she shouldn't say anything at all.

**5. When your boyfriend says he wants to move in, but you're not ready, you:**

A) Pick a fight. How could you move in with someone who still can't manage to clean the sink after shaving? You've asked him a million times. It's like he doesn't even care enough to try.

B) Throw him out. A window, the front door. Whatever's closest to the garbage.

C) Break up with him. Don't tell him why. You obviously want different things and talking about it will only muddy the waters.

D) Tell him yes, yes, a million times yes! Feel that pebble in your stomach grow into a boulder gathering speed down a hill toward an elementary school. Never voice your doubts or reveal your newfound anxiety-related constipation. It will only make him worry.

E) Tell him that his lease being up isn't a good reason to move in together. You told him you needed space after the miscarriage. No more secretly picking out names or looking up just how big it would be. A poppy seed. A blueberry. A green olive. You were going to throw away all your future plans for him and an apple seed. Without the apple seed, moving in together seems like a rash act. You haven't even known each other that long. Four months. You want to be smart. You hope he can respect that.

*Results:*

**Mostly A**
You may have some issues around impulsivity and aggression that you should look into with a qualified therapist.

**Mostly B**
Physical abuse isn't cute. Get yourself to anger management before a court mandates it!

**Mostly C**
Bottling up all your feelings isn't healthy, and hiding from the world won't solve your problems. You need to learn how to draw boundaries and ask for what you want.

**Mostly D**
There's something called "fawning" that you might want to look into. Stop catering to other people so much! You are responsible for your own happiness, not everyone else's.

**Mostly E**
Congratulations! You're basically a zen master! You don't need that lavender bubble bath, but maybe run it anyway? Check out this new bath bomb from our sponsor! You deserve it for dealing with A–D's bullshit.

# Gutter Ball

I probably shouldn't have come here. I'm not great with people, strangers. I'm told that I carry myself like a rich girl. You couldn't tell by looking at me that my dad grew up poor. Like didn't have enough food to eat poor. He collected bottles and cans and turned them in to buy candy bars. That's how he got diabetes. That's what killed him. Me, I don't have diabetes yet. I do have loose ligaments. Meaning my joints are too flexible and don't have a strong enough hold on my bones. I once dislocated my left hip. I couldn't tell you when or how. It just slipped out. I don't sense pain the way most people do. That's what chronic pain does. It gives you an inability to tell if you're in some pain when only big, life-threatening pain matters. And I'm completely out of shape. I haven't bowled in a decade. Not since college. I don't have the kind of friends who bowl. That's how I ended up in this Meetup of people in my age bracket bowling on a Sunday night. My trick is to hurl a light ball at a fast speed. It can bully the pins into falling. I don't have the muscle mass I used to for more technical aiming, so this is my best approach. I launch a ball down the lane. It thunks against the wood like I've murdered the ball and crashes into the pins, sending them flying into the air like a flight of swallows searching for safety. It's a strike. I'm not surprised. I usually get a strike first. The group is speechless before they burst into applause. They didn't expect someone like me to be able to do that. What they don't know is that I'll get progressively weaker through the night.

This will be my best showing. I don't tell anyone that my dad was a semi-pro—I mean, I think he was. I sort of remember my mom mentioning it, and he had a ton of trophies. We still have them in some forgotten spider-webbed corner of the basement. Mom's been careful not to throw away anything of his. He died when I was a teenager, so going through his stuff later in life might be my best way to get to know him, beyond my shitty memories. I can't figure out a way to tell these strangers about my dad without it coming out as bragging or opening up the conversation to my dead dad. So I carry his trophies strapped to my back during the conversation and pretend like I didn't spend a decent chunk of my childhood hours with him ignoring his advice and tossing a ball down the lane however I wanted. Everyone else is careful about letting the ball loose. None of them expected to be the worst player. That was supposed to be my job. I ask them about their actual jobs, their lives. Because if I can steer the conversation, then I can play keep away with my issues. They loosen up and bowl better. I become worse. I get a gutter ball. I never get gutter balls. I used to have this slight spin that I adjusted for by moving a little to the left, so the ball would hit the center pin from the side. The spin's gone now. My muscle memory is gone. Gutter ball. Gutter ball. Gutter ball. An inverse turkey. The group is baffled. The muscles in my wrist and shoulder are screaming. I explain loose ligaments. A guy says, "I get like that." I say, "Really?" He shrugs. He doesn't get like that. He's just trying to bond because I found his account-ing job *fascinating*, and he might want to fuck me. Soon my inner thighs and my back are added to the cacophony of voices. The more tired I get, the more frustrated I get, the more I think about my dad. How he bent me to his will. How he never—not once—asked about my joints. How we could've bonded if he hadn't been so intent on ordering me around. If only he'd seen me as a person and not an extension of him. My ball smacks the alley. It ends up in the gutter, and I sympathize. My body is vibrating in pain. The voices of agony blend together, so I can't focus on any one. Pain is the body's way of telling us to stop what we're doing. Fine, I tell myself. Okay. It's okay. We're okay. We don't have to do this anymore. We can rest now.

# Don't You Worry There's Still Time

Every Tuesday night at 7:15 my favorite bar plays "You Wouldn't Like Me" by Tegan and Sara. I go mostly so I can be transported back to my shitty college years. Really self-flagellate before my friends arrive. They're tired of me replaying events for the millionth time and making adjustments big and small. I have about fifteen minutes until they show, but I look around, just in case. That's when I see him. My ex-boyfriend. Daniel. Lounging by the fire like he has any business being in my small town when all he wanted was fame. New York. LA. Anywhere he could get paid to pose, maybe while saying words, for money.

The gap between us is closing. My feet are moving like I'm a fish that bit into a lure. I'm following where the line leads. Up close I can tell it's not Daniel. It's almost him. It's his doppelganger. His dark-haired, bearded doppelganger. And, okay, this guy's head is a little rounder and he's got a bit of a stomach, but I never cared about those kinds of things.

"Hey," I say. I hate the sound of my voice. Breathy and desperate.

The Tegan and Sara song starts with a chord strummed quickly twice, then again and again before the lyrics kick in. I flinch. Identifying with this song in front of him is humiliating. All my angst and self-loathing are floating on sound waves around us.

"Hi?" Not-Daniel says. He's clearly waiting for someone who's not me. The low lighting and the flicker of the fire make his face—the one I know so well—seem mysterious.

"Sorry to bother you," I say. "Do you mind if I sit with you while I wait for my friends? The last time I was here alone I got harassed, but you seem cool."

Even the way he bobs his head for yes is identical to Daniel. "Uh—sure," Not-Daniel says. He's unsure, but just as invested in outmoded, mostly symbolic chivalry as Daniel. He limply smiles. He's waiting for a woman.

I lean my elbows onto the table to get a better look. Same medium lips and same thick, non-arched eyebrows. His eyes even have the same lightning circle of white around the pupils. Unnoticeable unless you've really gazed into them searching for the mysteries they hold. But his beard is dark and Daniel's too lazy to dye his beard. That's how I know for sure he's Not-Daniel. They're like the Hitler clones in *The Boys from Brazil*. I picture an army of ex-boyfriends destroying cities with their behavioral indecision and insistence that The Shins are the greatest band ever.

I shake off that thought. "Where are you from?"

"Philadelphia."

So they're probably not related. "How'd you end up here?"

His face colors. The sign of a story, if there ever was one. "Needed a change."

"Kind of a random place."

"Yeah."

"I did the same thing," I offer. "It's a postcard town."

He looks at me funny like he knows what I'm talking about. I wonder if I'm the doppelganger of someone he once loved. If my questions are rattling him as much as his presence is rattling me.

"I mean look at this place," I say. "The dark brick, the beaten floors. If you scuffed the floor, nobody could tell because these floors are older than the country!"

Not-Daniel chuckles. "I'll tell my girlfriend. She likes factoids."

"What else does she like?"

He thinks. Really squints into the distance, like he's scanning the past for any detail he can grip onto. "Grilled cheese." Gross. "Martinis." Ick. "Always finishing the chapter of the book she's reading before taking a break." Respect.

"She sounds cool."

"She is."

"That's great," I say warmly. "It always speaks well of a man when he loves the person he's with."

His eyes bulge like my hands are around his neck. He tries to cover it up with a smirk at my over-stepping, but I've seen under the mask. He may be Not-Daniel, but he's still Daniel. "I think it's a little too early to say that."

"How long has it been?"

He scratches his neck beard. "Two months, officially."

"Unofficially?"

He shifts, says, "That's pretty personal," and gulps his beer.

"You're right," I say. "Sorry." Here I am apologizing to this motherfucker for something that isn't really my fault and certainly isn't something he understands. His entire life is a neck beard itch, and the women in his life watch for clues because they can't get the truth they crave instead. They'll never be satisfied.

"No worries," he says. "Hey, do you want a drink?"

The waiter drops off my blood orange cider, and I glance up at Not-Daniel. "Do you believe in fate?"

He smirks. "No."

"I do," I say, shrugging. "If only because it makes life a little more magical."

"So your life isn't magical?"

"Not generally, no."

He leans in and whispers, "Maybe you should do something about that."

My breath catches in my throat, and I choke on nothing. My body is panicking before my brain can follow. I become aware of the moisture collecting under my armpits. And the way he knows just how to make me feel like a piece of shit, I recognize that. I remember that.

His girlfriend arrives in a cloud of strong floral perfume. She looks like me—cranky and half-sure she's in the wrong place—but she's not me. I'd never call someone "babe," even if I was trying to claim a man. She's weary but jealous, and rightly. She knows she doesn't have him.

"Sorry, I didn't mean to interrupt your night," I say. "I just didn't want to wait alone."

My almost doppelganger nods skeptically as I rise to find a new seat. I order another cider and tap my knuckles against the table. That's when I notice. My song ended a while ago.

# If You Want It Bad Enough

I know what damaged girls look like. The white girl wasted, half-dressed mess in six-inch heels. A fresh cigarette between her fingers. She fucks randos and might be the Typhoid Mary of Chlamydia, but no one cares because she's such a good time and she never complains. Then there's me. Untrusting of strangers. Digging chocolate chip cookie crumbs out of my cleavage because that's what happiness tastes like. Perennially alone because I'm unwilling to take the same risks as everyone else. No one gives a fuck about me. Girls like me disappear.

The first shot feels like the fire I need to rebirth myself, so I choke down another. A third for good luck. Soon I'm engulfed in flames, surrounded by strangers. I forget myself. Talk loud. Belly laugh. Nuzzle up to some guy. We dance to the next song because I claim it's my favorite. There's no dance floor, but it turns out one can be made if you want it bad enough.

The room becomes a kaleidoscope of forgettable faces and splashes of color. My body is fluid in ways sober me could only fantasize about. I twist out of my winter coat and throw it in the general direction of our barstools. The crop top I bought for this night barely covers anything, but I'm so hot and dizzy. My shoulder knocks into a nearby group like I'm trying to break into a locked room. I bounce back, unsuccessful. Beer rolls across the floor in waves. Sorry, I say. It's not enough. I offer to buy their next round.

Some guy hustles me out the door. I rub my bare arms in the freezing night air. He comes back and throws my coat at me.

Fine! I scream. Fine!

I cackle and it rattles every cell in my body. I'm coming apart at my foundation. Sinking into the quicksand beneath. I struggle into my coat and peer inside the windows. People are unsure what I'm going to do next. Their apprehension travels on waves between us. The power to change their night thrums through my blood. I can feel it in my teeth, the ends of my hair. I stand up tall like a statue and grin, my bright red lipstick smeared down my chin. The people inside shudder and turn away.

Can you see me now?

# Notes and Acknowledgments

"Don't You Worry There's Still Time" is a lyric from the Tegan and Sara song "You Wouldn't Like Me."
"Through Rose-Colored Glasses" draws inspiration from Alex McElroy's "The Death of Your Son: A Flow Chart."

This chapbook wouldn't exist without the lovely people of Black Lawrence Press pulling it out of the slush during the Spring 2020 Black River Chapbook Competition. Thank you to Diane Goettel, Angela Leroux-Lindsey, and Gina Keicher for their work behind the scenes. To Zoe Norvell, who designed this lovely cover and its interior. Endless gratitude to Kit Frick for her patience and expertise as she shepherded me every step of the way.

When I started writing flash, Kathy Fish's Fast Flash class sent me off in the right direction. Having the doors opened to a new form by one of its leaders was a privilege. Thank you to Kathy Fish, Kim Magowan, and Francine Witte for blurbing this chapbook.

Many thanks to Bending Genres for hosting workshops that several of these stories were written and reworked in. Thanks to instructors Tara Campbell, Jonathan Cardew, Len Kuntz, Hillary Leftwich, Sabrina Orah Mark, Robert James Russell, Bud Smith, Nancy Stohlman, and Meg Tuite for their feedback and insight.

Lit mags give us a platform to share our stories, and I'll always be grateful to the places that have been such great homes for my work. In particular:

"Coming of Age" was previously published in *Jellyfish Review*.

"Don't You Worry There's Still Time" was previously published in *Ellipsis Zine*.

"Gutter Ball" was previously published in *matchbook*.

"Heirloom Seed Propagation" was previously published in *The Nottingham Review*.

"Household Extractions" was previously published in *Five on the Fifth*.

"The One That Gets Away" was previously published in *Jet Fuel Review*.

"Quiz: How Mature Are You?" was previously published in *McSweeney's Internet Tendency*.

"Through Rose-Colored Glasses" was previously published in *The /tɛmz/ Review*.

"We're Not Allowed Outside" was previously published in *Cleaver Magazine*.

"What the Detectives Found in Her Abandoned Car" was previously published in *Pithead Chapel*.

A huge thank you to flash fiction Twitter for being such a generous community of writers and readers. Without readership, writers are just people who tell themselves stories. This is more fun.

To Sarah, who I wouldn't be here without. My mother, who's always supported my writing, even when I didn't. And to George, who's always there.

**Chelsea Stickle's** flash fiction appears in *matchbook*, *Pithead Chapel*, *McSweeney's Internet Tendency*, and others. Her story "Postcard Town" was selected for *Best Microfiction 2021*. Other stories have been nominated for *Best Small Fictions*, *The Best of the Net*, *Best Microfiction*, and the Pushcart Prize. She lives in Annapolis, Maryland with her black rabbit George and a forest of houseplants. *Breaking Points* is her debut chapbook. Read more at chelseastickle.com and on Twitter @Chelsea_Stickle.